GEPT
新制全民英檢

初級 閱讀實戰力 Level Up!

試題本

Preface 序

　　全民英檢測驗 2021 年起全面調整初級、中級、中高級初試聽力及閱讀能力測驗的考題類型，旨在配合 108 年國教新課綱的核心素養教育理念。初級閱讀能力測驗中，第二部分「段落填空」新增選項為句子或子句的題型，以測驗考生理解文章脈絡與判斷前後文語意的能力，而第三部分「閱讀理解」新增多文本題型，以測驗考生面對多篇文章資訊的整合推論能力，問題類型亦新增圖片題。

　　本書針對閱讀能力測驗上述兩大題型 ——「段落填空」與「閱讀理解」，精心編寫六十篇切合新制考試方向的試題，包括十篇「段落填空」與五十篇「閱讀理解」。文本類型涵蓋傳統「單篇閱讀」四十篇及新制「多文本題型」二十篇，單篇閱讀再細分為主題多元豐富的「文章類」與題材包羅萬象的「生活類」，俾使讀者熟悉各種閱讀文本。

　　本書在試題本內特別就「閱讀理解」題型，整理英檢初級測驗常見的考題類型，每一類型皆詳述解題攻略並附上例題，以實務經驗手把手傳授作答技巧，幫助讀者提升能力。

　　詳解本除將所有試題精闢解析之外，「閱讀理解」更清楚標示考題類型，讀者按部就班演練並內化後，必能逐步培養堅實的應考能力，在實際考試中輕鬆拿高分。

　　祝大家學習成功！

Contents 目錄

🎯 閱讀理解測驗的閱讀與解題策略

一、閱讀文章前先快速瀏覽閱讀理解問題

閱讀理解測驗答題的第一步是先快速瀏覽文章後的題目，以了解稍後閱讀文章時需留意的重點及方向，回頭閱讀文章時便可快速掌握與題目相關的內容。

二、遇到難字時試著猜測字義或先跳過

閱讀文章時，若遇到不熟悉的單字或片語，可以隨手標示，並試著從上下文猜測它們的意思，如果一時無法猜測出來可先跳過，繼續往下閱讀，之後視答題需要再回頭判斷。這樣做的目的是讓閱讀過程流暢、不被干擾中斷，除較能掌握整篇文章的大意之外，也會有較多的作答時間。

🎯 閱讀理解測驗的問題類型與解題攻略

閱讀理解測驗的解題方式與問題類型有關，以下整理全民英檢初級常考的問題類型並分析個別的解題策略。

| 類型一 | 主旨題 | ➔ | 從拆解到統整 |

📑 **測驗重點** 掌握閱讀文本的主題與大意

🔍 **解題攻略**
   ❶ 拆解：找出各段落或篇章各部分的中心概念
   ❷ 統整：將各中心概念統整成通篇主旨

👁 **常見問題型態**

❶ What is this article mainly about?
本文的主旨為何？

What is the purpose of the article?
本文的目的為何？

What is the main idea / focus of the article?
本文的主要重點是什麼？

❷ Why did John / Daisy /... write this email? / Why has the email been written?
約翰 / 黛西 / ……為什麼寫這封電子郵件？ / 寫這封電子郵件的目的為何？

❸ What would be the best title for the article?
哪一項最適合做為本文的標題？

From:	Barbara <barbara.wu@yourmail.com>
To:	Mike <michael.chen@yourmail.com>
Subject:	Saturday's Picnic
Date:	Wednesday, June 10

Dear Mike,

I just emailed Sandra, and she said that everything is almost ready for our picnic this Saturday. She and Eric are bringing sandwiches and salads. Victor and Amy are bringing the barbecue food, and you and I are going to bring the drinks. We deserve a picnic after a hard week's work!

I think we should bring soft drinks, fruit juice, and beer. I know you guys like beer in summer! The girls don't drink beer, so we'll be happy with soft drinks and fruit juice.

Can you pick me up at 8:00 on Saturday? Please email me back ASAP!

Barb

Q1: What is the purpose of the email?

    A. To cancel an activity

    B. To invite a person to an activity

    C. To confirm the time of an activity

    D. To inform about details of an activity

解題方式：

拆解：

第一段：敘述野餐準備工作的分工方式

第二段：提及其中一項準備工作的細節

第三段：約定野餐當天的碰面時間

統整：

由以上各段重點得知，整封電子郵件主要是關於野餐準備工作的細部內容，故本題正確答案為 **D**。

📝 測驗重點　掌握及理解閱讀文本中的細部資訊

🔍 解題攻略

找出題目及各選項的關鍵字，並在閱讀文本中找到對應的字詞或文句，判斷選項的敘述正確與否。

👁 常見問題型態

❶ According to the article, which of the following is true?

根據本文，下列哪一項敘述正確？

What is most likely true about...?

關於……，哪一項敘述最有可能是正確的？

What is NOT true about...?

關於……，哪一項敘述不正確？

❷ What is NOT mentioned about... in the article?

關於……，本文未提及哪一項？

What information is NOT given in the article?

本文中沒有下列哪一項訊息？

例題一

（閱讀文本請見 p. iii 類型一例題）

Q2: Which is true about the picnic?

　A. Sandra is not going.

　B. There won't be beer.

　C. It'll be on the weekend.

　D. Eric is going to bring the drinks.

解題方式：

A 項：電子郵件內文第一段第一句敘述 Sandra 表示野餐的準備工作幾乎都已就緒，第二句敘述她會帶三明治和沙拉，可知她會參加野餐。　➲ 錯誤選項

B 項：電子郵件內文第二段第一、二句 Barbara 提到男生在夏天喜歡喝啤酒，但女生不喝，建議另準備不含酒精飲料，可知野餐會有啤酒。　➲ 錯誤選項

C 項：電子郵件的主旨 Saturday's Picnic 指出野餐的時間是星期六　➲ 正確選項

D 項：電子郵件內文第一段第二句敘述 Sandra 和 Eric 負責準備三明治和沙拉　➲ 錯誤選項

由以上分析可以得知 C 項為正確答案。

Q3: Which food or drinks will NOT be served at the picnic?

A.

B.

C.

D.

解題方式：

本題問野餐中不會出現哪一種食物或飲料，電子郵件內文第一段第二句敘述有人負責準備三明治和沙拉，第三句敘述有人負責準備烤肉食材以及飲料，第二段第一句建議飲料部分應準備無酒精飲料、果汁和啤酒，全篇未提到蛋糕，可知 **D** 項為正確答案。

📑 測驗重點 理解文句隱含的背後意義或弦外之音

🔍 解題攻略 在閱讀文本中找出與題目或選項相關的敘述，推敲其衍生的含意。

👁 常見問題型態

❶ What does the writer suggest in the article? / What is suggested in the article?

作者在文章中暗示哪一項？／本文暗示哪一項？

What can we know about...?

關於……，我們可以得知哪一項？

❷ According to the letter, what will John / Daisy /... most likely do next?

根據這封信，約翰／黛西／……接下來最有可能做什麼事？

What will happen...?

……將會發生什麼事？

例題

（閱讀文本請見 p. iii 類型一例題）

Q4: What do we know about these people?

A. They all like to drink beer.

B. Eric and Victor are brothers.

C. They have a picnic every month.

D. Barbara wants to go to the picnic with Mike.

解題方式：

A 項：電子郵件內文第二段第三句敘述參加的女生不喝啤酒 ➲ **錯誤選項**

B 項：電子郵件通篇沒有相關的敘述或暗示 ➲ **錯誤選項**

C 項：電子郵件通篇沒有相關的敘述或暗示 ➲ **錯誤選項**

D 項：電子郵件內文第三段第一句 Barbara 問 Mike 野餐當天是否可以去接她 ➲ **正確選項**

由以上分析可以得知 D 項為正確答案。

📑 **測驗重點**　將假設性情境與閱讀文本相關內容連結

🔍 **解題攻略**　在閱讀文本中找出與題目中假設的情境相關的敘述，連結後判斷答案。

例題

（閱讀文本請見 p. iii **類型一**例題）

Q5: One of Barbara's friends sent the following message to her:

> Hi, Barbara. I couldn't get any fish because they were sold out in the supermarket.
> Could you get some near your place?

Who might this person be?

A. Eric

B. Amy

C. Mike

D. Sandra

解題方式：

找出題目重點：

訊息傳送人說買不到魚，請 Barbara 協助採買。 ➲ 可知訊息傳送人負責採買魚

找出閱讀文本相關敘述：

根據電子郵件內文第一段第三句前半部，得知負責準備烤肉食物的人是 Victor 和 Amy。

綜合以上分析可以得知 **B** 項為正確答案。

📑 **測驗重點** 將不同閱讀文本中相互關聯的資訊整合並融會貫通

🔍 **解題攻略** 在閱讀文本中找出與題目相關且相互關聯的字句，整合後判斷答案。

例題

（閱讀文本第一篇請見 p. iii 類型一例題）

（閱讀文本第二篇）

> Dear Diary,
>
> I had a really good day today. The picnic was a lot of fun! It was nice that we had drinks other than beer. I really can't stand the smell of beer! I was glad that everyone else liked the light food I brought. The meat they prepared for the barbecue also tasted great, and I ate a lot. We were lucky that it didn't rain until we were going to leave. I went back home in Mike's car in the evening. I'm starting to look forward to the next picnic!

Q6: Who might be the writer of the diary?

A. Eric

B. Victor

C. Sandra

D. Barbara

解題方式：

本題問寫日記的人是誰，需先找出日記中的關鍵線索，再找出第一篇電子郵件中相應的訊息，兩篇文本相互關聯的訊息為：

	線索一	線索二	線索三
第二篇 （日記）	第三句： 有啤酒以外的飲料很不錯	第五句： 作者帶了輕食	第六句： 其他人準備了烤肉
第一篇 （電子郵件） 對應訊息	第二段第三句： 女生不喝啤酒，如果有無酒精飲料和果汁，她們會很高興	第一段第二句： Sandra 和 Eric 負責準備三明治和沙拉	第一段第三句： Victor 和 Amy 負責準備烤肉食材
⬇	⬇	⬇	⬇
結論	日記作者是女生 （排除 A、B 項）	日記作者可能是 Sandra 或 Eric （由線索一的結論得知可排除 Eric）	日記作者不可能是 Victor 或 Amy

由以上分析可以得知日記的作者是 Sandra，因此 C 項為正確答案。

寄件者：	芭芭拉 <barbara.wu@yourmail.com>
收件者：	麥克 <michael.chen@yourmail.com>
主　旨：	星期六的野餐
日　期：	六月十日 星期三

親愛的麥克：

我剛寄了電子郵件給珊卓，她說這星期六野餐的所有事都差不多準備好了，她和艾瑞克會帶三明治和沙拉過去。維克多和艾咪會帶烤肉的食物，我和你負責帶飲料。努力工作了一星期後，大家來野餐是應該的啦！

我想我們該帶點無酒精飲料、果汁和啤酒。我知道你們男生喜歡在夏天喝啤酒！我們女生不喝啤酒，所以如果有無酒精飲料和果汁，我們會很開心。

可以星期六早上八點來接我嗎？請盡快回信給我！

芭兒

Q1: 本電子郵件的目的是什麼？

　　A. 取消一項活動

　　B. 邀請某人參加一項活動

　　C. 確認一項活動的時間

　　D. 通知一項活動的細節

Q2: 關於野餐，哪一項敘述正確？

　　A. 珊卓不會參加。

　　B. 不會有啤酒。

　　C. 在週末舉行。

　　D. 艾瑞克會帶飲料。

Q3: 野餐中不會提供哪一項食物或飲料？

A. 　　B. 　　C. 　　D.

Q4: 關於這些人，我們得知哪一項？

A. 他們都喜歡喝啤酒。

B. 艾瑞克和維克多是兄弟。

C. 他們每個月都舉辦野餐。

D. 芭芭拉想和麥克一起去野餐地點。

Q5: 芭芭拉的一位朋友傳了以下訊息給她：

> 嗨，芭芭拉。我買不到魚，因為超市裡的魚賣完了。妳可以在家附近買嗎？

這個人可能是誰？

A. 艾瑞克

B. 艾咪

C. 麥克

D. 珊卓

（閱讀文本第二篇）

親愛的日記：

我今天過得真開心。野餐太好玩了！我們有啤酒之外的飲料真棒。我真的受不了啤酒的味道！我很開心其他人都喜歡我帶去的輕食。他們準備的烤肉也非常好吃，我吃了好多。我們運氣很好，直到我們要離開時才下雨。傍晚我搭麥克的車回家。我開始期待下次的野餐了！

Q6: 日記的作者可能是誰？

A. 艾瑞克

B. 維克多

C. 珊卓

D. 芭芭拉

Chapter 1 單篇閱讀 試題

Part A 文章類

Diet & Health 飲食與健康

三 段落填空

Bananas are eaten all over the world because they are delicious, healthy, and convenient. Usually, people only eat the __(1)__ of a banana. They throw away the peel, which is the yellow or green skin on the outside of the banana. __(2)__ This is because it contains many things __(3)__ are good for our blood sugar and heart health. Eating the skin also __(4)__ less waste. Banana skins, though, may contain bad chemicals. This means they must be washed very carefully before they are eaten. Baking or boiling them is a good idea, too. Even after cooking the skins, they may still be hard and taste bitter.

1. A. image   B. addition   C. inside   D. surface 表面

2. A. Bananas are now in danger from illness.
   B. Banana skins, though, create a lot of trash.
   C. Yet, we should eat many different kinds of fruit.
   D. However, some people say that we should eat the skin, too.

3. A. and   B. that   C. so   D. who

4. A. leads to 導致   B. takes away   C. makes up   D. deals with 處理

2

📖 閱讀理解

班尼迪賀

Eggs Benedict is a popular breakfast and brunch food. It is made with a round, flat 扁 bread called an English muffin, which is cut in half. Eggs and Canadian bacon are two other main elements. Finally, it is topped with hollandaise, 蛋黃油醋 sauce which is a mix of eggs, butter, and lemon juice. The history of eggs Benedict can be traced back 追溯 to the US in the 19th century. However, there are different opinions as to who invented the dish. Some say that a woman named Mrs. Benedict asked the cook at a New York restaurant to create something new for her in the 1860s. Others say that a man named Lemuel Benedict first ordered all the elements for eggs Benedict in a New York hotel in 1894. Whatever the truth of the matter is, eggs Benedict is enjoyed in lots of countries today. You can now also order many special types, which include everything from tomatoes and potatoes to fish.

1. Which of the following would be the best title for the article?
   A. The Story of a Popular Dish 熱門食物
   B. The Best Ways to Cook Eggs
   C. The Finest Brunches in the US 地的
   D. The Favorite Foods of Mr. Benedict

2. When was eggs Benedict first created?
   A. In a hotel in 1860
   B. In a restaurant in 1894
   C. In Canada in the 1900s
   D. We don't know for sure.

3. What is true of eggs Benedict?
   A. It is only made with bacon and eggs.
   B. It is only eaten in the United States.
   C. It is now available in different types.
   D. It is no longer as popular as it once was.

Sports & Fitness 運動與健身

三 段落填空

Not everyone likes to take part in organized team sports. Some people (1) to build exercise into their daily lives. One way to do this in Taipei, and other big cities in Taiwan, is to use a YouBike. This bicycle sharing service started in 2009. It allows people (2) a bicycle from one station and return it to any other station. This means it is very convenient. It is also very cheap and easy to use. (3) , too, as they are made by the respected Taiwanese company Giant. The YouBike system helps people to fit exercise into their day. (4) , they can ride a bicycle to or from school or work.

1. A. pause　　　　　B. promise　　　　C. progress　　　　D. prefer

2. A. renting　　　　B. to rent　　　　　C. rent　　　　　　D. and rent

3. A. The bicycles are of good quality
　　B. Running is an easy decision
　　C. The service stops on weekends
　　D. You should maintain your health

4. A. At last　　　　　B. Until now　　　　C. For example　　　D. On the contrary

📖 閱讀理解

Joining a gym can be expensive, but there are ways to get fit in our own homes. One such way is by an exercise called planking. This is a great way to help your shoulders, back, stomach, hips, and bottom become stronger. In fact, planking can be good for almost every part of your body. It can even help decrease back pain. However, it is very important to plank correctly so that you do not hurt yourself. First, you need to lie face down on the ground. Then, you raise yourself up so your lower arms are on the floor and your hands are in front of your face. Your back should be straight, and your legs should be raised off the ground with the help of your toes. The idea is to hold this position for as long as possible. Over time, you should be able to hold it for longer and longer. You should give planking a try today!

1. What is the main idea of the article?

   A. How and why to plank correctly   B. How planking became so famous

   C. Why gyms are great places to work out D. Why exercise is important for our bodies

2. Which of the following pictures shows the correct way to plank, according to the article?

   A.    B.

   C.    D.

3. How does the writer finish the article?

   A. By encouraging people to plank   B. By giving the history of planking

   C. By listing other popular exercises   D. By discussing the advantages of walking

Travel 旅遊

三 段落填空

Ireland is a country in western Europe. Its main city is called Dublin. Dublin is always busy, but if you visit in the middle of March, it is (1) busier than usual. (2) On this day, people fill the streets and have parties. They wear green clothes, (3) the color is closely linked with Ireland. They dance and sing traditional Irish songs, and they drink Guinness, which is a black beer that comes from Dublin. All of this is done (4) St. Patrick, who was an important person in the Church of Ireland. The day is also celebrated all over the world, especially in the US.

1. A. even   B. very   C. most   D. again

2. A. The reason for this is not fully understood.
   B. That is because March 17th is St. Patrick's Day.
   C. This is mainly true in the first half of the month.
   D. There is a lot of bad weather at this time of year.

3. A. if   B. though   C. once   D. as

4. A. in case of   B. in charge of   C. in memory of   D. in favor of

閱讀理解

The national flower of Japan is the cherry blossom. The appearance of these beautiful pink and white flowers used to tell farmers when to plant their vegetables. Now, the flowers mean hope, life, and spring to the Japanese. Citizens of the country even have parties and picnics under cherry blossom trees when the flowers are about to appear. Visitors, too, travel to Japan in April just to see the beautiful flowers. However, in 2021, the flowers arrived in March. In fact, in the city of Kyoto, they appeared earlier than at any time since the 15th century. Experts say that this is because of climate change. This is the heating of the planet that is blamed on human activity. Warmer temperatures mean that spring arrives earlier and the flowers come out earlier. They also mean that visitors wishing to see Japan's cherry blossoms might need to book an earlier trip in the future.

CH 1

1. What is the main focus of the article?
   A. The loss of a highly popular tree
   B. The warm summer weather in Japan
   C. The reasons for the picnic habit in Japan
   D. The early appearance of a famous flower

2. According to the article, why do visitors go to Japan in the spring?
   A. To help out on farms
   B. To learn about Kyoto
   C. To look at beautiful views
   D. To enjoy the cool weather

3. Which of the following is explained in this article?
   A. Why a Japanese tradition disappeared
   B. Why something took place in Japan in 2021
   C. Why temperatures are getting colder on Earth
   D. Why Japanese people changed a habit in 2021

News Reports 新聞報導

三 段落填空

    Tatler is the name of a famous British magazine. It is also printed with different articles in Taiwan and other Asian countries. In 2021, many of the writers chose their favorite cities for food in Asia. __(1)__ That is because the food in Taipei is of good quality and is easy to find. *Tatler*'s article __(2)__ the city for its mix of local, national, and international food. It also __(3)__ several places for special praise. These include the large fish market in Zhongshan, the tea restaurants in Maokong, and the dumplings at Din Tai Fung. And of course, no discussion of Taipei's food would be complete __(4)__ the traditional night markets.

1. A. The article can also be viewed on the internet.
   B. Sadly, they rated Taipei's food as lacking in taste.
   C. All of them agreed that Bangkok was by far the best.
   D. Along with Tokyo, Seoul, and others, Taipei was on this list.

2. A. directs   B. provides   C. admires   D. requires

3. A. picks out   B. cares for   C. leaves out   D. figures out

4. A. including   B. to include   C. and include   D. without including

閱讀理解

Many people these days use their phones all the time. They even play games and send messages on their phones while they walk the streets. This can be dangerous, and some people have walked into things and hurt themselves. Paeng Min-wook, a design student from South Korea, has invented an item that could stop this from happening. It is called The Third Eye. It is a round ball that can be fixed to the center of your head, above your real eyes. When you lower your neck to check your phone, The Third Eye "opens." If it senses you are about to walk into something, an alarm goes off. However, Paeng does not really think that The Third Eye is a solution to people using their phones at the cost of their safety. Rather, he wants people to hear about The Third Eye and realize that they should put their phones down more often. He joked that if they don't, humans will need a real extra eye in the future.

1. What would be the best title for this article in a newspaper?
   A. *Student Invents The Third Eye*   B. *Eye Game Becomes Popular*
   C. *The Third Eye Operation Successful*   D. *Student Hurt While Using Phone*

2. Which picture correctly shows the style and position of The Third Eye?

   A.   B.

   C.   D.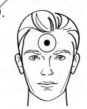

3. What does Paeng want to achieve?
   A. People using their phones less   B. An increase in jokes about eyes
   C. An increase in the cost of phones   D. Millions of sales of The Third Eye

Unit **5**

Family 家庭

三 段落填空

Who makes the meals in your family? Perhaps it's your mom, who gets home from the office before anyone else. Perhaps it's your dad, who no longer works. Maybe you even do the cooking yourself. If you want to give the cook a (1) , though, you could always ask a robot to do it. A company (2) Moley Robotics has created a "robot kitchen." The robot can take items from the refrigerator, use the range and the kitchen sink, and serve dishes. It can even do the washing-up. (3) This high price means you might have to (4) your mom and dad's cooking for a while longer.

1. A. limit   B. break   C. mark   D. reason

2. A. is called   B. calls   C. called   D. to call

3. A. It turns itself off when finished.

    B. What it can't do is buy the food.

    C. However, the meals don't taste good.

    D. However, it costs around NT$10 million.

4. A. put up with   B. run out of   C. take care of   D. do away with

閱讀理解

When you think of the word "family," you probably think of your parents and brothers or sisters. That is, you think of human families. However, animals have families, too. And just like in human families, the older members give the younger members advice and help. Take sperm whales, for example. These large sea animals were often hunted and killed during the 19th century. However, a study by The Royal Society shows that the whales learned how to avoid the hunters' weapons. The older, more experienced whales then taught the younger ones where to swim to get away from the hunters. The hunters were therefore able to kill far fewer whales. Very few countries now support the killing of whales. These clever animals, therefore, may now be able to pass on different information to their families. Scientists hope that whales can learn the positions of all the trash in the oceans. If the older whales can teach the younger ones how to avoid this trash, more families of whales will be saved.

1. Which of the following is the primary focus of this article?
   A. A study into small sea animals
   B. An animal that no longer exists today
   C. An animal that learned to avoid danger
   D. A family of hunters in the 19th century

2. What did the older whales do when they were hunted?
   A. They swam away from their families.
   B. They asked the younger whales for help.
   C. They gave up and were caught by the hunters.
   D. They passed on knowledge to younger whales.

3. What do scientists hope whales will do today?
   A. Stop leaving their families
   B. Help to clean up the oceans
   C. Teach other animals fun tricks
   D. Learn how to keep away from garbage

 段落填空

If you were asked to name a famous Taiwanese movie director, you would probably say Ang Lee. He has made great films _(1)_ *Brokeback Mountain* and *Life of Pi.* _(2)_ One such director was Edward Yang. Yang was brought up in Taipei and then traveled to the US to study. When he realized that he wanted to make films, he came back to Taiwan. Most of his movies are set in cities. They deal with _(3)_ like the conflict between the traditional and modern worlds. Perhaps his most famous film is *Yi Yi*, _(4)_ about a middle-class family in Taipei. It won lots of major prizes.

1. A. along with   B. thanks to   C. rather than   D. such as

2. A. In fact, the history of Taiwanese movies can be traced back to 1901.

    B. However, there have been many other successful directors from Taiwan.

    C. On the other hand, the director has spent most of his adult life in the US.

    D. At the time of this writing, Ang Lee has directed fourteen successful movies.

3. A. topics   B. opinions   C. projects   D. memories

4. A. which   B. is   C. which is   D. that is

12

📖 閱讀理解

Children across the world have enjoyed reading stories about Paddington Bear for over sixty years. A British writer named Michael Bond created the character in the late 1950s. Paddington is a talking bear. He wears an old hat and a thick coat and carries a travel bag. In his first story, he is found at London Paddington train station by a family called the Browns. He goes to live with the family and has lots of fun times. He is a very kind bear, but he often gets into trouble and has to work hard to get out of it. Kids love the stories about Paddington Bear because he is cute and funny. Adults can safely read the stories to their children because good always beats evil. There are other ways to experience the stories, too. There are several television shows about Paddington Bear. There are some successful movies as well. And there is a lot of information about the character at the Museum of London.

1. Based on the article, what does Paddington Bear look like?

A.

B.

C.

D.

2. What is NOT true about Paddington Bear?

    A. His story is based on the life of a train driver.

    B. Children can learn good things from his stories.

    C. Children like him because he makes them laugh.

    D. He is a bear that always thinks about others' feelings.

3. Which way of enjoying the Paddington Bear stories does the article focus on?

    A. The books   B. The movies   C. The museum   D. The TV shows

三 段落填空

Starting school can be exciting for young children. It provides a chance to be in a different environment and learn new things. However, for some, starting school for the first time can be hard. They may feel __(1)__ about being away from their parents. They may worry about meeting new children and making new friends. __(2)__ Moms and dads can find __(3)__ hard to leave their children in the care of someone else. It might be the first time they have had to do this. Starting school, __(4)__, is a natural part of life. It is the beginning of a fun, new chapter in the lives of children and their parents.

1. A. tired   B. nervous   C. lucky   D. excited

2. A. There are ways to make this simpler.
   B. The teachers can help during this time.
   C. On the other hand, parents find it easy.
   D. It can also be a difficult time for parents.

3. A. this   B. them   C. it   D. one

4. A. though   B. finally   C. therefore   D. especially

14

閱讀理解

When we are at school, we are taught that certain things are true. We are told that these are facts and that they are correct. However, when more information is discovered, sometimes "facts" can change. For instance, you may have been told that the Great Wall of China can be seen from space. It used to be said that the wall was the only object made by man that was like this. People who have traveled to the moon or into space, though, say this is not true. From space, the wall just mixes into the countryside around it. Another "fact" that has changed is also to do with space. Generations of children have been told that there are nine planets. Pluto, the furthest from the sun, was said to be the ninth. Scientists, though, have discovered more information. They now consider Pluto too small to be a planet. Thus, there are just eight main planets.

1. What would be the primary purpose of reading the article?

    A. To understand that facts can change

    B. To encourage people to become teachers

    C. To realize that traveling into space is hard

    D. To learn that information always stays the same

2. Why can't the Great Wall of China be seen from space?

    A. Parts of it have been moved.

    B. There is too much bad weather.

    C. It gets lost in the area around it.

    D. The wall is shorter than we thought.

3. What does the writer suggest in the article?

    A. We should try to discover facts on our own.

    B. Pluto is now the furthest planet from Earth.

    C. A new planet has been found in place of Pluto.

    D. We shouldn't believe everything we learn at school.

Shopping 購物

三 段落填空

Some people love shopping; others hate it. But we all have to do it, __(1)__ it's buying food, clothes, or even other less important items. When the world was hit by COVID-19, many people were unable to shop in traditional stores. Rather, they had to buy their goods on the internet. Millions of people, especially in the west, have continued to use Amazon for this __(2)__ for years. It is available in over fifty countries. Although Amazon can ship some goods to Taiwan, there is no Amazon Taiwan. Therefore, __(3)__ to buy things on the internet. These and many other companies saw their orders __(4)__ quickly in Taiwan during COVID-19.

1. A. though   B. until   C. whether   D. after

2. A. comment   B. instant   C. growth   D. purpose

3. A. it is not possible to buy everything that people need in Taiwan

     B. Taiwanese people use companies such as PChome and Shopee

     C. there has been a push for Amazon to sell more items in Taiwan

     D. people in Taiwan ask relatives in other countries to send them goods

4. A. increase   B. increased   C. to increase   D. have increased

📖 閱讀理解

　　This is a story about Tom. Tom was a 15-year-old boy who lived with his parents. His mom and dad did everything for him, including cooking, cleaning, and shopping. Tom never had to lift a finger. One day, though, Tom's mom and dad were both ill. Tom's mom asked him to go to the supermarket to do the food shopping. She told him to get three apples, five carrots, two bottles of juice, and some bananas. She asked him to write a list, but Tom said he was confident he could remember everything. However, when he got to the supermarket, Tom struggled to remember what his mom had said. Was it five apples and three bottles of juice? Or was it five bananas and three carrots? In the end, Tom bought five apples, three carrots, three bottles of juice, and some bananas. When he arrived home with the shopping, Tom's mom just rolled her eyes. Tom realized that he needed a lot more practice helping out around the house!

1. Which of the following would be the most fitting title for the story?
   A. *A Boy Learns a Lesson*　　　　　B. *A Boy with a Great Memory*
   C. *A Serious Illness in the Family*　　D. *A Family Trip to the Supermarket*

2. Why did Tom not write the food items on a list?
   A. He couldn't find a pen and paper.　　B. He wanted his father to go with him.
   C. He was sure he wouldn't forget them.　D. He planned to order them on the internet.

3. Which of the following shopping lists shows what Tom should have bought?
   A.
   ```
   Shopping List
   · 5 apples
   · 3 carrots
   · 3 bottles of juice
   · bananas
   ```
   B.
   ```
   Shopping List
   · 3 apples
   · 5 carrots
   · 2 bottles of juice
   · bananas
   ```
   C.
   ```
   Shopping List
   · 5 apples
   · 2 carrots
   · 3 bottles of juice
   · bananas
   ```
   D.
   ```
   Shopping List
   · 3 apples
   · 3 carrots
   · 2 bottles of juice
   · bananas
   ```

Unit 9 Leisure Activities 休閒活動

≡ 段落填空

Free time is very important in our lives. The activities we do outside of school or work can have a big (1) on our health and happiness. These activities might include playing sports, meeting family and friends, or just watching TV. A recent study 近期研究 suggests that young men spend more time on fun activities than young women. The study looked at nearly 900 Spanish people (2) 18 to 24. It found that men have 113 minutes of free time every weekday, (3) women have 101 minutes. (4) , but it adds up to 52 hours every year.

1. A. target   B. value   C. effect   D. method

2. A. aged   B. aging   C. who age   D. whose age

3. A. because   B. or   C. so   D. while

4. A. Children will be included in the next study
   B. This might not sound like much of a difference
   C. Women have to do more jobs around the house
   D. This is because men have many different interests

閱讀理解

There are many things that can affect our choice of free-time activities. One of these, of course, is our own personal interests. Another is how light or dark it is outside. For instance, you may enjoy running, but you do it more during the summer when the evenings are lighter. In around 70 countries in the world, the governments make sure that the evenings are even lighter during the summer. They do this by using daylight saving time. This means that the clocks are moved forward one hour in spring and then put back one hour in the autumn. In the US, it is commonly described as "spring forward, fall back." The result is that countries—mainly in North America and Europe—give their people an extra hour of natural light in the evenings to enjoy their free time. Daylight saving time was first introduced in the UK and US for a reason quite different from today. It was to save energy during the First World War.

1. Why is running talked about in the article?

    A. It is an example of a very healthy free-time activity.

    B. It is an activity that can only be done during the summer.

    C. It is an example of an activity that can be affected by the light.

    D. It is an activity that is enjoyed in some countries more than others.

2. What is the writer's personal opinion of daylight saving time?

    A. Every country should use it.

    B. It should be used all year round.

    C. It is a mistake that should be stopped.

    D. No personal opinion was given in the article.

3. Why was daylight saving time first introduced?

    A. To confuse the enemy during a time of war

    B. To give people more time to enjoy themselves

    C. To make different countries follow the same time

    D. To stop people using as much energy during a war

Office Life 職場面面觀

三 段落填空

Starting a new company can be expensive. There are lots of things to spend money on, from workers to tools. Many new small companies are choosing to __(1)__ money by not having a fixed office. In place of this, they use what is called a coworking space. This is a room or a building __(2)__ workers from different companies can share office space. In Taiwan, lots of new businesses are started every day. __(3)__ In Taipei, for instance, coworking spaces can be found in Xinyi, Songshan, and Daan, among other areas. Not only __(4)__ a good way to save money, but they also provide opportunities to meet people in your own and other industries.

1. A. provide   B. cash   C. deliver   D. save

2. A. that   B. what   C. where   D. which

3. A. Therefore, these spaces are becoming very common.
   B. However, there are none of these spaces in Taiwan.
   C. Still, goods are exported to many different countries.
   D. As a result, the roads are being improved in the cities.

4. A. do they   B. are they   C. is there   D. be there

📖 **閱讀理解**

Julie has always wanted to be a journalist. Ever since she was a little girl, she has dreamed of interviewing famous people and writing reports about important events. She studied to be a journalist for four years in college. While she was there, she wrote articles for the student paper. It took Julie nearly a year to find a job after graduation, but she finally got a position as a reporter at a local newspaper. On her first day, she was introduced to the chief reporter, an old man with glasses. He asked Julie to interview a singer who was visiting their town. Although not a fan of popular music, Julie was sure she knew what the young singer looked like. When she arrived at the meeting place, Julie started questioning the long-haired guy with a beard who was standing to her right. It was only after the fifth question that she realized the singer was the short-haired man with no beard who was standing on her left! Luckily, both the singer and the chief reporter saw the funny side and didn't blame her!

1. Which of the following facts about Julie is NOT true?

    A. She found a good job as soon as she completed her studies.

    B. She was a writer at a newspaper when she was in college.

    C. She liked the idea of being a journalist when she was a child.

    D. She wouldn't describe herself as being interested in popular music.

2. Which of the pictures shows the singer that Julie should have interviewed?

    A.    B.    C.    D.

3. What lesson might Julie have learned from her first day at the newspaper?

    A. She should listen to more rock music.

    B. She should get her hair cut more often.

    C. She should prepare more before an interview.

    D. She should go back to university to take another degree.

NOTE

Chapter 1 單篇閱讀 試題

Part B 生活類

Unit 11 Schedules & Timetables
時間表與時刻表

A

Amy & Sam's Vacation Plan

Day	Time of Day	Activity
Monday	Morning	Arrive at the hotel
	Afternoon	Go swimming at the beach
	Evening	Meal at a steak restaurant
Tuesday	Morning	A trip to see mountain lions
	Afternoon	Go walking in the countryside
	Evening	Go dancing at a local bar
Wednesday	Morning	Rest in the hotel
	Afternoon	Go swimming in the hotel pool
	Evening	Meal in the hotel restaurant
Thursday	Morning	A trip to see a local church
	Afternoon	Gift shopping in local shops
	Evening	Meal at an expensive restaurant

1. On which day will Amy and Sam spend the most time at their hotel?

   A. Monday

   B. Tuesday

   C. Wednesday

   D. Thursday

2. Which of the following is NOT true about Amy and Sam's vacation?

   A. They will spend some time by the coast.

   B. They will play a sport with local people.

   C. They will visit an important local building.

   D. They will go to see some animals in the hills.

3. When will Amy and Sam most likely buy presents for their friends?

   A. On Tuesday evening

   B. On Monday morning

   C. On Thursday afternoon

   D. On Wednesday afternoon

B

Train Schedule

Place	Train 1A	Train 2B	Train 3C	Train 4D
Great Town	07:47	08:53	09:25	10:01
Church Hill	07:57	09:03	09:35	10:11
Hazel River	08:00	09:06	09:38	10:14
Springfield	08:15	09:21	09:53	10:29
Capitol City	08:35	09:41	10:13	10:49

➤ *Changes to train times:*

- *The second train of the day is canceled because of a lack of customers.*
- *The third train of the day no longer stops at Church Hill.*
- *All trains will arrive at Capitol City ten minutes late because of track repair work.*

1. Which train will go straight from Great Town to Hazel River?

   A. Train 1A

   B. Train 2B

   C. Train 3C

   D. Train 4D

2. Why will Train 4D arrive at Capitol City at 10:59?

   A. There are too many people wanting to travel.

   B. There are more stops being added after Springfield.

   C. There are not enough workers to sell tickets at the station.

   D. There are delays because work is being done on the track.

3. James boards the train at Great Town. His office is a fifteen-minute walk from Springfield. Which train does James have to take if he wants to get to the office before 10 o'clock?

   A. 07:47

   B. 08:53

   C. 09:25

   D. He can't catch any train.

Chat Rooms 聊天室

Ⓐ

Jenna ⟨ Hi, Eric! How was your first day at the new school?

It was OK, thanks. The teachers and the classmates were all welcoming, but I miss my old friends. ⟩ **Eric**

Jenna ⟨ We miss you, too! School's not the same without you. What am I going to do in science class without you there helping me?

I know it's not your best subject, haha! I can still help you, though. Ask me anything here if you need me. ⟩ **Eric**

Jenna ⟨ Thanks, Eric. You're the best!

1. What do we learn about Jenna and Eric?

   A. They are classmates now.

   B. They have never met before.

   C. They used to date and were a couple.

   D. They no longer attend the same school.

2. What is Eric's opinion of his new school?

   A. He thinks everyone is friendly.

   B. He thinks the work is too hard.

   C. He thinks the people aren't nice.

   D. He thinks it has too many students.

3. Why is Jenna pleased with Eric?

   A. Because he is going to visit her

   B. Because he promises to help her

   C. Because he tells her she is clever

   D. Because he answered a hard question

B

Wally	Welcome to our music group!

Thank you! ▷ **Olivia**

Wally	If you have any questions, please let me know.

Actually, I was wondering if you guys ever meet up in person to listen to music together. ▷ **Olivia**

徐有覺得怪怪的

Wally	Not really, no. We just use this room to talk about our favorite artists and introduce new music to others.

OK, thanks. What are your favorite types of music, Wally? ▷ **Olivia**

Wally	I love hard rock and heavy metal. What about you?

I like all kinds of music! ▷ **Olivia**

1. Who most likely is Wally?

    A. The brother of Olivia

    B. A famous music artist

    C. The leader of the group

    D. A new member of the group

2. What do we find out about the group?

    A. It does not meet in person.

    B. It doesn't accept new members.

    C. It has been recently formed. 最近成立

    D. It focuses on one type of music.

3. What is true about Wally's tastes in music?

    A. He enjoys easy-listening music.

    B. He likes certain types of music. 某些

    C. He enjoys his own band's music.

    D. He likes different kinds of music.

A

Sandtown Movie Theater Presents

TWO MATCHES MADE TO LAST

Screen: Number Two

Seat: Number 7A

Admit One

Adult Price: $10 / Child Price: $7 / Student Price: $6 / Senior Price: $5

Please note that smoking is not allowed in the movie theater.

Please turn your phone on silent before the start of the movie.

Please take away your trash at the end of the movie.

You are not allowed to record any part of the movie—

anyone caught doing so will be told to leave the movie theater.

---

1. What do we learn about Sandtown Movie Theater?

   A. It has more than one screen.

   B. It is the only theater in town.

   C. It only shows one movie at a time.

   D. It does not allow eating or drinking.

2. Kerry goes to the local university. How much does she have to pay to see a movie?

   A. $5

   B. $6

   C. $7

   D. $10

3. Based on the ticket, why might you be told to leave the movie theater?

   A. You have created too much garbage.

   B. You have smoked outside the theater.

   C. You have been caught talking to your friend.

   D. You have been discovered recording the movie.

B

The Super American Football Center

LEA TOWN LIONS vs. CLINT CITY CATS

Friday, November 5th, 2021

7:30 p.m.

Section B / Line 10 / Seat 18

Admit One

Standard Price: $50 / Member Price: $30

Notes:

The Super American Football Center advises arriving half an hour before game time.

Members are asked to show their member card along with their ticket in order to be

charged the lower price.

No outside food or drinks are allowed in the center.

1. What is NOT true about the football game on the ticket?

　A. People will sit in different sections.

　B. It takes place on a weekday evening.

　C. People are advised to arrive at 7:30 p.m.

　D. The teams have names based on animals.

2. How can someone pay thirty dollars to see the game?

　A. Win a prize

　B. Arrive early

　C. Buy two tickets

　D. Become a member

3. Based on the ticket, what can people probably do if they want to eat food at the game?

　A. Order it from a restaurant

　B. Bring it from their own home

　C. Get it from inside the sports center

　D. Buy it from a food truck outside

Emails 電子郵件

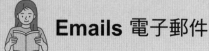

A

> From: office.manager@karens.kitchens.com
>
> To: office.staff@karens.kitchens.com
>
> Subject: Please Clean Up
>
> ---
>
> Hi All,
>
> Firstly, the cleaner has asked me to remind you that it is not her job to wash your dirty dishes. Please do not leave half-empty coffee cups or half-eaten sandwiches on your desks. These might encourage insects. The cleaner is here to empty the trash and make sure the shared areas are clean. Secondly, the parking lot will be closing early tonight at 6 p.m. Please make sure that you leave before this time.
>
> Thank you.
>
> Leah Vincent

1. What is the main topic of the email?
   A. The hiring of a new cleaner
   B. A new coffee shop in the area
   C. A message to keep the office clean
   D. The problems in the office parking lot

2. What is one of the cleaner's jobs?
   A. Washing dirty dishes
   B. Taking the trash away
   C. Cleaning the parking lot
   D. Cleaning everyone's desks

3. Why are insects discussed in the email?
   A. The company sells them as food.
   B. There are many in the parking lot.
   C. They might enter the office to eat the food.
   D. The office used to have a problem with them.

B

From:	p.simpson@coldmail.com
To:	g.flanders@zmail.com
Subject:	Hey!

George!

Long time no see, buddy! I don't think I've seen you since Barry's wedding ten years ago. I was looking through the photos the other day, and I realized we hadn't spoken for a while. So, I decided to email you to see how you're doing. Are you still living in California? How are Maggie and the kids? I got a new job as a house painter! I got tired of working in an office and wanted a change. Look forward to hearing from you.

Pete

1. What caused Pete to email George?

   A. He wanted to offer him a job.

   B. He needed to ask him a favor.

   C. He saw him in some old photos.

   D. He wanted to invite him to a wedding.

2. What does Pete NOT ask George about?

   A. His work

   B. How he is

   C. His family

   D. Where he lives

3. What do we learn about Pete?

   A. He is going to California.

   B. He is married with children.

   C. He has recently changed jobs.

   D. He needs to get his house painted.

Advertisements & Flyers 廣告與傳單

A

Sunnytown High School proudly presents our yearly...

SCHOOL FAIR! 園遊氏

Run by the students

Open to students, teachers, and the public

Friday, June 25th, 2021

1 p.m. to 5 p.m.

Come along and buy everything from homemade cakes
and local ice cream to classic novels from our library

All money raised will go to local homeless people—
a cause that was chosen by the students themselves

Spend some money, buy nice things, and help the
homeless at Sunnytown High's School Fair!

1. What information is NOT given in the reading?

   A. The name of the school

   B. The prices of the items to be sold

   C. When the school fair will be held

   D. Who has organized the school fair

2. What can you NOT buy at the school fair?

   A. Sweet goods made at home

   B. Books provided by the school

   C. Drinks provided by local firms

   D. Cold treats from local companies

3. Where will the money raised from the fair go?

   A. To people who have an illness

   B. To students from poor families

   C. To support the high school library

   D. To people who don't have a home

B

> # It's the grand opening of
> ## FANTASTIC FURNITURE
> ## on Saturday, August 7th, 2021
>
> You can find our store on Main Street, next to Paulie's Pizzas
>
> Our usual opening hours will be 9 a.m. to 6 p.m.
>
> But on August 7th, we'll be open from 7 a.m. to 7 p.m.
>
> And, if you're one of our first fifty customers, you'll get
> 10% off everything you buy!
>
> We sell locally made tables, cabinets, and closets—
> plus beds imported from Europe
>
> Come visit us on Saturday!

1. What will be different about Fantastic Furniture's first day?
   A. It will only sell certain items.
   B. It will close earlier than usual.
   C. It will open for longer than usual.
   D. It will give free pizza to customers.

2. How can shoppers save money on the opening day?
   A. Make a post on social media
   B. Arrive earlier than most people
   C. Write a review on the internet
   D. Spend a certain amount of money

3. How are the store's beds different from its other items?
   A. They are part of a special offer.
   B. They are not yet available for sale.
   C. They are made outside of the country.
   D. They are made from a different material.

Letters & Postcards 信件與明信片

A

Dear Sir,

I ordered some goods from your company, Super Prices, on December 10th. Based on your promise, all items should arrive in 48 hours. However, it is now December 17th, and they still haven't arrived. I understand that this is a busy time for your internet company, as many people are ordering presents for Christmas, but this kind of delay is not OK. I still want my goods, but I also want money off my next order.

Yours truly,

Bert Gentry

1. What is the main purpose of this letter?

   A. To judge

   B. To praise

   C. To welcome

   D. To complain

2. How many days late are the goods?

   A. Two days

   B. Five days

   C. Seven days

   D. We do not know.

3. Why is it currently a busy period for Super Prices?

   A. It is the rainy season.

   B. They are having a sale.

   C. It is the holiday season.

   D. They have fired workers.

B

To: Ms. Emma Chou
50, Shunli St., Taipei, Taiwan

Hi, Grandma!

Mom and Dad finally allowed me to go on vacation with my friends, and we're having a great time here in Florida. I'm writing this on the balcony of our hotel room. We had a fun day seeing all the people dressed up as cartoon characters and going on the rides at Disney World. Now, we're taking a rest before we go out for dinner. I'm going to have steak tonight! I can't wait to show you all my photos when I get home!

Lots of love,
Belinda

xxx

1. Who is Belinda on vacation with?
   A. Her friends
   B. Her parents
   C. Her co-workers
   D. Her grandmother

2. What do we know about Belinda?
   A. She does not eat meat.
   B. She is scared of flying.
   C. She stays at a hotel during the vacation.
   D. She has been to Florida with her parents before.

3. What is Belinda probably going to do next?
   A. Visit a very famous park
   B. Watch cartoons with friends
   C. Go to a restaurant for a meal
   D. Show a relative some photos

Questionnaires & Surveys 問卷調查

A

A Great Experience with Calvin's Rent-A-Car
Please fill out the form below.

- What is your name?

  Roger Moran
  _____

- How did you find out about us?

  My friend told me about your company.
  _____

- How would you grade the service? 評分

  ☐ 1 (very poor) ☐ 2 ☐ 3 ☑ 4 ☐ 5 (excellent)

- How would you grade the price?

  ☐ 1 (very poor) ☑ 2 ☐ 3 ☐ 4 ☐ 5 (excellent)

- How likely would you be to suggest us to your friends?

  ☐ 1 (very unlikely) ☐ 2 ☑ 3 ☐ 4 ☐ 5 (very likely)

---

1. What do we learn about the company on the form?

   A. It rents out cars.

   B. It sells used cars.

   C. It is a new business.

   D. It employs Roger's friend.

2. What does Roger think of the service at Calvin's Rent-A-Car?

   A. It is good.

   B. It is closer to being bad than good.

   C. It requires a great deal of work.

   D. It is less important than the cost.

3. Would Roger say good things to his friends about Calvin's Rent-A-Car?

   A. No, certainly not.

   B. The chance is 50-50. 半的意思

   C. Yes, without a doubt.

   D. The information is not given.

B

Why are you leaving?

1. What is your name?

   Melissa Barr

2. How long have you worked for the company?

   Over nine years

3. Which department did you work in?

   I first worked in buying, and then in marketing.

4. Why did you decide to leave the company?

   I feel like I need to test myself in a different field.

5. What was the best part about working for the company?

   Working with lots of great people in different departments

6. What was the worst part about working for the company?

   The managers would not change to modern working practices.

---

1. Why has Melissa filled out this form?

   A. She has quit her job.

   B. She is applying for a job.

   C. She is borrowing some money.

   D. She has bought something new.

2. What is NOT true about Melissa?

   A. She wants to change to a new career.

   B. She worked in two different departments.

   C. She was a manager in the buying department.

   D. She worked at the company for nearly ten years.

3. What does Melissa consider a negative part of working for the company?

   A. There was too little space.

   B. There were too many tests.

   C. The people were not friendly.

   D. The managers were too traditional.

Invitations & Cards 邀請函與卡片

A

Edward & Jennifer Clinton
and
Conrad & Elaine Kennedy

invite you to attend
the wedding of their children

Gareth Clinton
and
Sophia Kennedy

on Saturday, June 11th, 2022

The service will take place at 1 p.m. at
New Church, Forest Road, Darlington

The wedding party will follow at 3 p.m. at
Bartle Hall, Wood Road, Darlington

Gareth and Sophia ask that you do not bring gifts

Formal clothes are required

1. Who will Edward Clinton become on the day of the wedding?
   A. Elaine's husband
   B. Gareth's father-in-law
   C. Jennifer's ex-husband
   D. Sophia's father-in-law

2. What will happen at 3 p.m.?
   A. The guests will arrive at the church.
   B. The guests will get ready to have a big meal.
   C. Gareth and Sophia will start to open their gifts.
   D. Gareth and Sophia will become husband and wife.

3. Based on the invitation, which of the following is true?
   A. The wedding will be on the weekend.
   B. The hosts will only accept small gifts.
   C. The guests aren't required to wear formal clothes.
   D. The guests are advised to have lunch before the wedding.

B

Dear Hilary,

I was really sorry to hear about your accident. At your age, you really shouldn't be climbing so high, though! You should have hired someone to paint the house for you! You were so lucky that your grandson happened to drive by your house and saw you lying on the ground. I hope your leg and arm get better soon. I will come to visit you in the hospital as soon as I get back from my summer trip next week. I'm sorry I can't visit you sooner.

Get well soon!

Dennis

1. What happened to Hilary?

   A. She fell while painting.

   B. She caught a serious illness.

   C. She was hurt in a car accident.

   D. She got lost climbing a mountain.

2. Why does Dennis talk about Hilary's grandson?

   A. The grandson is a painter.

   B. The grandson saved Hilary.

   C. The grandson caused an accident.

   D. The grandson thinks Hilary is lying.

3. Why hasn't Dennis visited Hilary yet?

   A. He is on vacation.

   B. His car broke down.

   C. He hurt his leg and arm.

   D. He is in another hospital.

Price Lists & Menus 價目表與菜單

A

Carol's Cleaning Company Price List	
Service	**Price**
Kitchen – standard clean	$40 every hour
Kitchen – heavy clean	$60 every hour
Bathroom – standard clean	$50 every hour
Bathroom – heavy clean	$70 every hour
One-bedroom apartment	$90 every hour
Two-bedroom apartment	$90 every hour
Three-bedroom apartment	$90 every hour
Small house	$100 every hour
Large house	$120 every hour
Garage	$40 every hour

Please note:

Carol's Cleaning Company will refuse to clean your home if there is any danger to our workers.

1. Which is the most expensive service that Carol's Cleaning Company provides?
   A. A clean of a big house
   B. A heavy clean of a kitchen
   C. A clean of a large apartment
   D. A heavy clean of a bathroom

2. What can we learn about the company?
   A. It charges by the hour.
   B. It employs only one cleaner.
   C. It cleans homes and businesses.
   D. It has been around for ten years.

3. Laura wants to use the services of Carol's Cleaning Company. There are two bathrooms that require a heavy clean in her house. How much would it cost her every hour?
   A. $100
   B. $120
   C. $140
   A. $160

B

Mia's Coffee Shop
❧ Menu ❧

❋ First Course

Garden Salad	$8
Ham Salad	$10
Bread & Butter	$5

❋ Soup

Tomato Soup	$7.50
French Onion Soup	$9.50
Beef Soup	$11.50

❋ Main Course

Egg on Toast	$12
Fried Chicken	$14.50
Turkey Sandwich	$15.50

❋ Dessert

Chocolate Cake	$10
Apple Pie	$11.50
Ice Cream	$7.50

❋ Drink

Hot Black Coffee	$4.50
Hot White Coffee	$5.50
Iced Green Tea	$5

Please note: A service charge of 10% will be added to your bill.

1. What is NOT true about Mia's Coffee Shop?
   A. It offers three kinds of hot drinks.
   B. It offers more than one type of salad.
   C. It offers one soup that includes meat.
   D. It offers more than one choice of dessert.

2. What does the message at the bottom of the menu mean?
   A. The coffee shop will only accept cash.
   B. The coffee shop would like you to tip the waiters.
   C. The coffee shop would welcome any notes or comments.
   D. The coffee shop will include another charge on your bill.

3. Todd buys a ham salad and a chocolate cake. What is the total bill?
   A. $18
   B. $20
   C. $22
   D. $21.5

Guides & Maps 指引與地圖

A

Bobby,

I hope you're looking forward to the trip! I should arrive at the camping ground at 10 a.m. on Friday. As you'll arrive later than me, I'm leaving you a map showing you how to get there. Park your car in the parking lot at the bottom of Great Hill, and set off walking. Make sure you pick the safest path!

Ronald

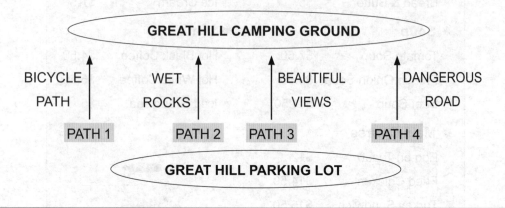

1. Why is Ronald leaving a map for Bobby?

   A. Ronald is playing a joke on Bobby.

   B. Bobby is not traveling with Ronald.

   C. Bobby has a poor sense of direction.

   D. Ronald is worried Bobby will be late.

2. How will Ronald travel to the parking lot?

   A. By car

   B. On foot

   C. By bicycle

   D. We do not know.

3. Which path will Bobby probably take to the camping ground?

   A. Path 1

   B. Path 2

   C. Path 3

   D. Path 4

B

Dear students,

Please see below the floor plan of the school.

CLEANING ROOM	GIRLS' RESTROOM	BOYS' RESTROOM		LUNCH ROOM	PRINCIPAL'S OFFICE
ENGLISH ROOM	HISTORY ROOM	GEOGRAPHY ROOM	MAIN HALL	BIOLOGY ROOM	PHYSICS ROOM
MATH ROOM	ART ROOM	COMPUTER ROOM		GYM	

Please note: The gym will be closed for repair work from February 1st to February 10th. Gym classes will move to the main hall. Any events that were to take place in the main hall during this time will be canceled.

1. Which of the following is true about the school?

    A. The art room is next to the history room.

    B. The English room is across from the math room.

    C. The geography room is next to the girls' restroom.

    D. The cleaning room is across from the computer room.

2. The school planned to hold a music show in the main hall on February 5th. What will happen to that show?

    A. It will not take place.

    B. It will take place in the gym.

    C. It will take place in a new hall.

    D. It will be changed to February 10th.

3. Jill is in one of the classrooms. The classroom is between two other classrooms, and there are no restrooms across from her classroom. Which classroom is she in?

    A. The English room

    B. The biology room

    C. The art room

    D. The geography room

NOTE

Chapter 2

多文本閱讀

試題

MIXED WEATHER FOR WEEK AHEAD

By Andreas Jones

Weather Reporter

The mixed weather we've been experiencing will continue into next week. You will need to have everything from sun hats to rain jackets at the ready! Monday and Tuesday will be very hot, with high temperatures of 29ºC. A cold front means the temperature will drop to 19ºC on Wednesday, but the weather will still be dry. The heavy rain will arrive on Thursday, and the temperature will drop by a further three to four degrees. At least there won't be any snow next week!

Dear Diary,

I was really looking forward to our school trip to the farm today. I wanted to see the cows and feed the lambs. However, our teacher told us that we couldn't go because of the bad weather. I don't know why we couldn't just take our umbrellas and carry on with the trip. We might get a bit wet, but that's no big deal. When it was canceled, I thought we might at least do something fun in class—play games or watch a movie. But we just did our usual subjects. I hate bad weather!

Zosia

1. What is NOT true about the week's weather?

    A. Tuesday will be as hot as Monday. ✓

    B. Thursday will be colder than Tuesday.

    C. Wednesday will be colder than Thursday.

    D. Monday will be warmer than Wednesday.

2. How did Zosia feel when she wrote her diary?

    A. She was excited to have seen some animals.

    B. She was looking forward to a coming activity.

    C. She was embarrassed to get all wet in the rain.

    D. She was sad about something that didn't happen.

3. On which day did Zosia write her diary?

    A. Monday

    B. Tuesday

    C. Wednesday

    D. Thursday

HELP WANTED!

We are a busy restaurant in the center of Manhattan, and we're looking for a cook to join our kitchen team. We require that you:

- Have attended cooking school in the US
- Have worked in a kitchen before
- Are able to work lunch and dinner times
- Are able to deal with a busy kitchen environment

You will be paid $20 an hour, and you will get two days off each week.

For more information and to apply, please visit:

www.rheasrestaurant.com

RHEA'S RESTAURANT
JOB FORM

Date: *07.08.2021*

Name	*Anthony Ramsay*
Email	*tonyram@coldmail.com*
Education	*I studied for three years at Cumbria Cooking School in the UK.*
Current Position	*Cook at Morgana's Restaurant, New York*
Date Available	*August 1st, 2021*
Times Available	*(Please underline)* Breakfast <u>Lunch</u> <u>Dinner</u>
Personal Comment	*I am an excellent cook with experience in another busy New York restaurant. Although I like my current job, I want to push myself further, make new dishes, and work with new people. I am available for an interview right away.*

1. What is the purpose of the first reading?

   A. To find someone to cook for a school

   B. To search for a cook who stole money

   C. To find someone to work in a restaurant

   D. To search for someone to clean a kitchen

2. What do we know about Anthony?

   A. He has career goals.

   B. He is married to Morgana.

   C. He wants to earn more money.

   D. He doesn't like working weekends.

3. Why might Anthony NOT get the job at the restaurant?

   A. He cannot work at breakfast time.

   B. He cannot start work straight away.

   C. He didn't go to an American school.

   D. He doesn't have enough experience.

TV GUIDE

Time	Channel	Program	Information
8 p.m.	Channel 10	*Fly Away Today*	A show following one man's travels around the world
	Channel ABC	Movie: *Sooner or Later*	A will-they-won't-they love story about a couple from different countries
10 p.m.	Channel 10	*Music Is My Life*	The beautiful story of a child's love of music
	Channel ABC	Movie: *One of Us Must Know*	This ghost movie will make you feel scared and keep you up at night!

Saturday, August 21st (table title)

Daisy   Where are you? It's almost 7:30.   7:27 p.m.

7:31 p.m.   Sorry. The team and I were discussing the game.   **Joe**

Daisy   When will you be home? 7:32 p.m. The movie starts at 8:00.

7:36 p.m.   Probably not till 8:15. Sorry I can't make it. How about the one at 10:00? I can watch that with you.   **Joe**

Daisy   I don't want to be frightened and have bad dreams! I want to watch the one we agreed on: the love story!   7:37 p.m.

7:45 p.m.   OK, whatever you want.   **Joe**

1. What is NOT true about the TV programs tonight?

    A. There's more than one movie.

    B. There's a program about birds.

    C. One of the programs is about music.

    D. The TV guide lists programs on two channels.

2. What do we know about Daisy and Joe?

    A. They don't live together.

    B. Daisy likes travel stories.

    C. Daisy doesn't like frightening movies.

    D. Joe is going to stay at his friend's house tonight.

3. Which TV program did Daisy and Joe agree on?

    A. *Fly Away Today*

    B. *Sooner or Later*

    C. *Music Is My Life*

    D. *One of Us Must Know*

From: adam.richards@richards-motors.com

To: all.staff@richards-motors.com

Subject: Company Barbecue

Hi,

I would like to invite you all to a barbecue at my house this Saturday starting at 2 p.m. It is my way of saying thank you for your hard work during these past few months. It has been one of our busiest periods, and I'm proud of how well we've handled it. No one needs to bring any food or drink. My wife will prepare a salad, my son will make pizza, my daughter will make dessert, and I'll cook the meat. I hope to see everyone there!

Adam

Elaine Hey, Jan. Are you feeling OK after this afternoon's barbecue? 10:05 p.m.

10:06 p.m. Not really. I've got stomachache. **Jan**

Elaine Me, too! I think it was the cream cake. I thought the cream smelled bad at the time. 10:06 p.m.

10:07 p.m. I knew I shouldn't have eaten it, but I was being polite. **Jan**

Elaine At least the weather was nice and sunny. I had good fun in the pool. 10:08 p.m.

10:08 p.m. Yeah, that was great. There wasn't much to drink, though. How can he only offer Coke and water? **Jan**

Elaine Beats me! I'll take my own next time! 10:09 p.m.

1. What do we learn about Richards Motors?

   A. It is doing well.

   B. It is closing early.

   C. It is losing money.

   D. It is hiring new workers.

2. What else do Elaine and Jan complain about besides the cake?

   A. The pool

   B. The people

   C. The weather

   D. The drink selection

3. Who prepared the food that Elaine and Jan think made them ill?

   A. Adam

   B. Adam's son

   C. Adam's wife

   D. Adam's daughter

A Note to Our Guests

We hope you are enjoying your stay at the Happy Healthy Hotel. Some of our services will need to close briefly for repair work. Please see the table below for further information. 短暫地

Happy Healthy Hotel—Repair Work	
Date	**Area Affected**
July 14th	Inside pool
July 15th	Gym
July 16th	Outside pool
July 17th	Bar & restaurant

To apologize for any trouble, we are offering guests 50% off a two-night stay in our sister hotel, the Feeling Fine Hotel, which looks over the river.

From:	jim.hsieh@coldmail.com
To:	pam.lien@coldmail.com
Subject:	Thanks

Dear Pam,

Thank you so much for giving me a birthday I will never forget. I wasn't expecting that at all! The meal in the hotel restaurant was excellent. I don't think I've ever eaten such perfectly cooked fish! It was nice to sit by the pool, too, although I was sad that the outside pool was closed. I'm looking forward to our stay in the Feeling Fine Hotel. Thanks again.

Jim

1. How is the Happy Healthy Hotel saying sorry to its guests?

   A. By taking them on a boat trip along the river

   B. By offering them a free meal at the restaurant

   C. By offering them a cheaper stay at another hotel

   D. By taking money off their bill at the Happy Healthy Hotel

2. What do we learn about Jim and Pam?

   A. Jim is a better swimmer than Pam.

   B. Pam surprised Jim with the hotel stay.

   C. Pam and Jim are brother and sister.

   D. Jim and Pam prefer the Feeling Fine Hotel.

3. When did Jim and Pam visit the Happy Healthy Hotel?

   A. On July 14th

   B. On July 15th

   C. On July 16th

   D. On July 17th

Seaton High School welcomes parents and families to our...

Sports Day!

All of our students have been training hard for their events and are looking forward to showing off to their moms and dads. Please see below for the list of events.

Seaton High School Sports Day	
Time	Event
1:00 p.m.	100-meter race
1:30 p.m.	500-meter race
2:00 p.m.	Long jump
2:30 p.m.	High jump

Free drinks and snacks are available in the school lunch room.
These have been kindly provided by a local company.

From: ninarobertson123@coldmail.com

To: principal@seaton-high-school.com

Subject: Sports Day

Mr. Skinner,

I am writing this email to say thank you for a successful and well-organized sports day. My husband and I took the afternoon off work to watch our daughter Lisa take part in—and win!—the 100-meter race. We stayed for the whole afternoon and really enjoyed it. All of the other parents, family members, and students seemed to be having a great time, too. And the juice and the lemon cake were delicious!

Thanks again.

Nina

1. What do we know about the food at the sports day?

    A. The food was quite expensive.

    B. The food was provided by a local business.

    C. The students made the food by themselves.

    D. The food was sold at stands around the playground.

2. What is true about Nina?

    A. She attended the sports day alone.

    B. She didn't try the free juice or cake.

    C. She left right after her daughter's event.

    D. She used personal leave to attend the sports day.

3. What time was Nina's daughter's event?

    A. At 1:00 p.m.

    B. At 1:30 p.m.

    C. At 2:00 p.m.

    D. At 2:30 p.m.

THE GREAT GAMES STORE

New Games Available on September 27th	
The Lost Darkness	An exciting game set in a future when the sun never goes down
Faster, Faster, Faster 5: Don't Stop	The latest racing game on the most popular tracks
To The Death	Fight insects from space in this fun new fighting game
Super Sports Fun	Try your hand at a range of different sports in this new game

Please note that on the first day, we will only have 100 copies of each game in store. More will be available in the following days.

NEW GAME REVIEW

By Max Mitchell

Games Reporter

My son has been looking forward to getting a new video game for his game machine, and he loves fighting games. I, on the other hand, have been excited for months about the new racing game. I've played and completed the earlier four games, and I hoped that the new one would not let me down. And it didn't! The **graphics** are excellent. Everything on the screen looks very real. It's also nice to race around different tracks and in different places. I am now looking forward to the next one!

1. What is true about The Great Games Store?

   A. It sells over one hundred different games.

   B. It mainly sells fighting and sports games.

   C. It won't sell the new games until October.

   D. It only has a limited number of the new games.

2. What does "**graphics**" in Max's review probably mean?

   A. People who make a computer game

   B. Pictures shown on a computer screen

   C. The tracks based on a computer racing game

   D. Images shown on a computer game box

3. Which game did Max review?

   A. *The Lost Darkness*

   B. *Faster, Faster, Faster 5: Don't Stop*

   C. *To The Death*

   D. *Super Sports Fun*

West City Hospital

Visitors Policy

Rule 1	Visits are allowed from 2 p.m. to 4 p.m. and 6 p.m. to 8 p.m. on weekdays, and 8 a.m. to 8 p.m. on weekends.
Rule 2	All visitors must report to the main desk in the department they wish to visit and get a visitor's pass.
Rule 3	Please wash your hands before going in to see the patient.
Rule 4	Please do not sit on the patient's bed.

Please note: Hospital parking is limited.
Visitors are advised to use other means.

Fred I went to see Chris in the hospital this morning. 8:30 p.m.

8:31 p.m. How is he? I haven't gone to see him yet. I've got stomachache. **Jenna**

Fred He is recovering from the operation quite well. Something strange happened, though. One of the nurses asked me to leave! 8:31 p.m.

8:33 p.m. Did you go there outside of visiting hours? **Jenna**

Fred No. She said I shouldn't sit on Chris's bed because of hospital rules. She was quite serious. 8:34 p.m.

8:35 p.m. I guess they've got these rules to keep the patients safe and healthy. **Jenna**

Fred You should remember that when you go visit him! 8:36 p.m.

1. What are visitors to West City Hospital advised NOT to do?

   A. Drive to the hospital

   B. Bring a gift for the patient

   C. Visit on weekday evenings ✓

   D. Stay for longer than one hour

2. What do we know from Fred's and Jenna's messages?

   A. Chris's health is improving.

   B. Jenna is going to the hospital the next day.

   C. Fred visited the patient during the wrong hours.

   D. Chris is staying at the hospital because of a stomachache.

3. Which hospital rule did Fred break?

   A. Rule 1

   B. Rule 2

   C. Rule 3

   D. Rule 4

Hi, Ben,

I'll be home late tonight. A woman from the office is leaving today, so we're all going out for a meal with her after work. Your dad will be late, too, as he needs to work late. Please use one of the food ordering apps on the iPad to order yourself some dinner. Don't spend over $10, and try to order something with some vegetables! Remember to do your homework, and don't have any wild parties!

Love, Mom

FFF: Fast Fresh Food Straight to Your Home!		
Menu		
Item	**Information**	**Price**
Beef Sandwich	Toasted sandwich with beef and cheese	$10
Pizza Surprise	Pizza with lots of vegetables	$7.50
Chicken Noodles	Hot noodles with chicken	$9.50
Super Vegetables	A black rice dish with cream and vegetables	$12.50

Please note:

· An extra charge of $2 will be added to each order.

· We promise the food will arrive within 40 minutes.

· If we fail to deliver your food within 40 minutes, you will get 25% off your next order.

1. Why will Ben's mom be late home?

   A. She is leaving her job today.

   B. She is going out with Ben's dad.

   C. She has to work late in the office.

   D. She is going out with friends from work.

2. Ben's food took one hour to arrive. What will Ben get?

   A. A special free dessert

   B. A message saying sorry

   C. Money off his next order

   D. His money back for the order

3. According to Ben's mother's advice, what should Ben order?

   A. Beef Sandwich

   B. Pizza Surprise

   C. Chicken Noodles

   D. Super Vegetables

REPORT CARD

Name of Student: Emma Aceveda

Subject	Grade	Comments
English	A	Emma continues to be an excellent student, getting top grades for all of her papers. It's clear she loves reading.
History	D	Emma did really well in this class last year, but this year the quality of her work has started to go down.
Art	D	Emma tries her best, but it seems she is not a natural artist.
Math	B	Emma has dealt well with the difficult work this year. She can work out the answers quickly in her head.

Dear Mrs. Aceveda,

Your daughter Emma is always very polite and friendly. She comes to class on time and always hands in her homework on time. She seemed to be really interested in the topics we studied last year and always got high grades. However, this year, she is getting poor grades. I am not sure if she is not interested in what we're studying, or if there are problems at home or with her friends. Please let me know when you are free to come to the school to discuss this with me.

Thank you.

Mr. Vendrell

1. What do we know from Emma's school report?

   A. Emma is interested in art.

   B. Emma gets top grades in English.

   C. Emma struggles to do math in her head.

   D. Emma got different grades in all the four subjects.

2. What does Mr. Vendrell NOT suggest might be Emma's problem?

   A. She might have lost interest in the subject.

   B. She might have difficulties with her friends.

   C. She might be having trouble with her parents.

   D. She might be finding the lessons too difficult.

3. Which subject does Mr. Vendrell teach?

   A. English

   B. History

   C. Art

   D. Math

Study Desk 405

You should have received the following items:

· 1 large desk top

· 1 desk back

· 4 desk legs

· 1 raised computer screen table

· 8 large nails

· 4 small nails

Please follow these steps:

1. Lay the desk top on the floor and use 4 large nails to fix the desk legs.

2. Use the other 4 large nails to fix the desk back.

3. Turn over your desk and stand it on the ground.

4. Use the 4 small nails to fix the raised computer screen table.

Please note that Study Chair 405 must be bought separately.

From: keith.cotton@zmail.com

To: customer-service@desksareus.com

Subject: Study Desk 405—Order Number DSD4051287

Dear Customer Service,

I recently ordered the above item from your online store. It arrived quickly and was packed well. When I fixed the legs to the top of the desk, it was clear that the quality of the wood was very good. However, when I began to fix the desk back to the main part of the desk, I realized that the other four large nails were missing. Could you please send these out to me as soon as possible?

Thank you.

Keith Cotton

1. What is true about Study Desk 405?

    A. It comes in different colors.

    B. It is supplied with an office chair.

    C. It comes with a small raised table.

    D. It is supplied with a set of drawers.

2. Which part of Study Desk 405 does Keith NOT say positive things about?

    A. The cost of the items

    B. The speed of the order

    C. The safety of the packing

    D. The quality of the material

3. Which step of the guide was Keith unable to complete?

    A. Step 1

    B. Step 2

    C. Step 3

    D. Step 4

Job Interviews for Assistant Manager

Monday, October 18th

Time	Name	Comments
09:00	Tasha Rodriguez	Has a master's degree in business studies, but no real-world experience
09:30	Neil Imperioli	Used to be a manager for a huge clothes company, but now wants a lower-stress job
10:00	Pia Delaney	Is currently an assistant manager at another computer firm like ours, but is looking to move somewhere new
10:30	Vernon Falco	Has worked in this company for years and is looking to earn more money

From: ssullivan@placer-computers.com

To: ecooper@placer-computers.com

Subject: Today's Interviews

Hi Emily,

Sorry to email you so early, but I wanted to let you know that I will miss one of the interviews today. I have an important meeting with the director of sales at 10:30, so I will need to give the last interview a miss. However, I'm sure that you are more than able to do the interview on your own. I hope your visit to the dentist went well, by the way. Let's go out for lunch when I've finished my meeting.

Sylvie

1. What is correct about the people who have applied for the job?

    A. Pia Delaney does not work in the industry.

    B. Neil Imperioli would like to be a manager.

    C. Tasha Rodriguez has never had a job before.

    D. Vernon Falco works for a clothes company.

2. What do we know about Emily?

    A. She will cancel her visit to the dentist.

    B. She will meet the director in place of Sylvie.

    C. She won't be able to have lunch with Sylvie.

    D. She receives Sylvie's email on the interview day.

3. Whose interview will Sylvie miss?

    A. Tasha Rodriguez's

    B. Neil Imperioli's

    C. Pia Delaney's

    D. Vernon Falco's

SuperShop Department Store		
Floor Guide		
Floor	**Store Information**	**Other Information**
1F	Rings & watches, glasses & sunglasses, pictures & gifts, ladies' & men's shoes, children's shoes, bags & purses	Ladies' restroom, information desk
2F	Ladies' formal clothes, ladies' informal clothes, men's formal clothes, men's informal clothes, sports goods, summer clothes	Ladies' & men's restrooms
3F	Children's clothes, children's toys, kitchen items, bedding & towels	Family restroom
4F	Western & Asian restaurants, wine shop, movie theater	Ladies' & men's restrooms

Gabriel Have you finished yet? I want to go up to the fourth floor and get something to eat. 3:42 p.m.

3:44 p.m. Not yet. I'm looking for new T-shirts for Matthew. He's already grown out of those ones we got him for Christmas. Then, I want to get a new cover for his bed. **Olivia**

Gabriel We've been in here for hours! 3:45 p.m.

3:48 p.m. Why don't you go downstairs and look for some new golf clubs? **Olivia**

Gabriel I don't need any. 3:49 p.m.

3:53 p.m. OK, I'll try to be quick. **Olivia**

Gabriel Thank you. I get to pick the restaurant! 3:53 p.m.

1. Which of the following items could you buy on the first floor?

    A. A nice bottle of red wine

    B. A new towel for the beach

    C. A watch for a special birthday

    D. A man's suit for an important event

2. What do we know about Olivia and Gabriel?

    A. They both need new T-shirts.

    B. They have a son named Matthew.

    C. They prefer western to Asian food.

    D. They are shopping for Christmas presents.

3. Which floor of the department store are Olivia and Gabriel currently on?

    A. The first floor

    B. The second floor

    C. The third floor

    D. The fourth floor

https://www.student-paper.com   — ☐ ✕

STUDENT ELECTION ENDS IN SURPRISE

The student government election ended in surprise late last night as Diana Garcia was elected head of the government. Miss Garcia received 41% of the vote. The person in second place—third-year student Miguel Rivera—received 33%. It was widely believed that Mr. Rivera, the most popular one in the election, would win. Many students admitted to not knowing who Miss Garcia was. However, she gained a lot of support on social media in the days leading up to the election. The other two students—Albert Nguyen and Elora Torres—each got 13% of the vote.

Dear Diary,

I woke up this morning and saw the election results online. "Surprise" didn't come close to describing how I felt. I had never even heard of Diana Garcia until last week, and now she's going to be the head of the student government! She got over 40% of the vote, while my guy only got a third. I hope Diana Garcia has got some good policies rather than just an ability to make eye-catching posts on social media. Only time will tell, I guess.

Helen

1. How did Diana Garcia probably win the election?

   A. By delivering a funny speech

   B. By coming up with great policies

   C. By giving free cakes to the students

   D. By becoming popular on social media

2. Why did Helen write in her diary?

   A. To express her joy

   B. To say she is sorry

   C. To express her doubts

   D. To say she was wrong

3. Who did Helen vote for in the student government election?

   A. Elora Torres

   B. Diana Garcia

   C. Miguel Rivera

   D. Albert Nguyen

https:// www.nightbikerides.com

The Best Night Rides in Hope Town

Bicycle rides at night are popular during the summer because of the cooler evening temperatures. Let's look at four of the best in Hope Town.

Ride A This takes you up into the hills to get a great view of the city.

Ride B This easy ride takes you along the town's beautiful river.

Ride C This ride takes you through the city's busy streets—why not stop for a drink or snack along the way?

Ride D This difficult ride takes you on a trip through the woods.

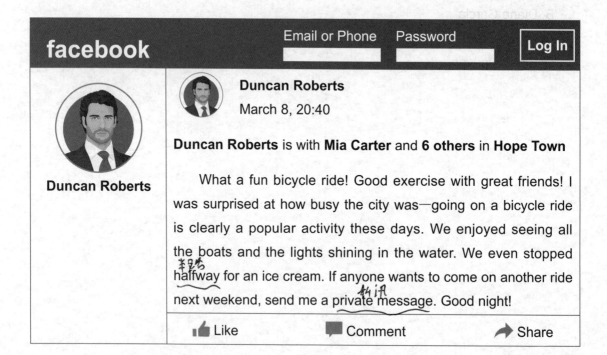

facebook

Email or Phone   Password   **Log In**

Duncan Roberts
March 8, 20:40

Duncan Roberts is with **Mia Carter** and **6 others** in **Hope Town**

Duncan Roberts

What a fun bicycle ride! Good exercise with great friends! I was surprised at how busy the city was—going on a bicycle ride is clearly a popular activity these days. We enjoyed seeing all the boats and the lights shining in the water. We even stopped halfway for an ice cream. If anyone wants to come on another ride next weekend, send me a private message. Good night!

👍 Like   💬 Comment   ➤ Share

1. What does nightbikerides.com say about summer night rides?

   A. They are easier than day rides.

   B. The weather isn't as hot at night.

   C. They don't require bicycle lights.

   D. The summer months are less popular.

2. What does Duncan NOT say in his Facebook post?

   A. Bicycle rides are a good way to make friends.

   B. There may be another ride next week.

   C. There were more people than he expected.

   D. They enjoyed a sweet treat during the ride.

3. Which ride did Duncan and his friends go on?

   A. Ride A

   B. Ride B

   C. Ride C

   D. Ride D

CH
2

TOY WONDER WORLD

GRAND SALE!

To celebrate the opening of our new store, we are having a grand sale!
See below for our best deals!

Item	Was	Now
Animal Puzzle—put together this picture showing the animals of the world	$19.99	$9.99
Be A Soccer Star—everything you need to be a great player	$29.99	$14.99
Dino the Dog—this cute little toy dog acts just like a real pet!	$39.99	$19.99
Total Turtles—one of today's most popular video games	$49.99	$24.99

Dear Grandma Alice and Grandpa Pete,

I am writing this note to say thank you very much for my birthday present. I love it! Mom and Dad won't let me have a pet because they say I don't know how to look after one. So, this is the next best thing! I will take him everywhere I go, just like a real dog. This way, I can show them that they can trust me to look after a real dog, too!

Lots of love,

Timmy

1. What is true about the sale at Toy Wonder World?

    A. It only lasts for one week.

    B. It only includes animal toys.

    C. It is because a store is closing.

    D. Its best deals are all half price.

2. Why does Timmy talk about his parents in the note?

    A. They want to say thank you.

    B. They want to return the gift.

    C. They won't let him have a pet.

    D. They made him write the note.

3. How much did Grandma Alice and Grandpa Pete spend on Timmy's gift?

    A. $9.99

    B. $14.99

    C. $19.99

    D. $24.99

Welcome to
Music Conversations!

We're the online room for all music lovers.
Please follow the rules of the room, as listed below.

Rule 1: Do not use the room to run your own business or sell your own products.

Rule 2: Do not send any message that includes bad language.

Rule 3: Do not ask for the full name or address of any other member of the group.

Rule 4: Do not attack anyone personally for their opinions.

Anyone found to be breaking these rules will be asked to leave the room and will not be allowed back for a period of one month.

Debra Hey! Has anyone in here listened to the new Bruno Mars album? 8:30 p.m.

8:31 p.m. Of course! He's my favorite singer. **Chris**

Debra Cool. He's mine, too! What do you love about him? 8:31 p.m.

8:35 p.m. I like the way his music mixes many different styles like rock and soul. What about you? **Chris**

Debra I love the words in his songs. They mean a lot to me. 8:36 p.m.

8:36 p.m. Maybe we could meet up and listen to him together. What's your last name, Debra? Where do you live? **Chris**

Debra I don't think that's such a good idea. Maybe we should stop talking. 8:38 p.m.

1. What happens if you break a rule of the online room?

   A. You can't come back at any point.

   B. You can't come back for a few weeks.

   C. You have to pay a fine to the manager.

   D. You have to say sorry to other members.

2. What does Debra like about the singer's songs?

   A. The way the music is written

   B. The way different styles are mixed

   C. The way the words are written

   D. The way the songs make her dance

3. Which rule did Chris break?

   A. Rule 1

   B. Rule 2

   C. Rule 3

   D. Rule 4

Real Town Airport – Flights Leaving		
Time	To	Flight No.
16:40	Tokyo	IT 6834
17:10	Manila	PA 9821
17:40	Seoul	IT 1348
18:10	Kuala Lumpur	KL 4492

Passengers are advised to check the weight limits with their airline. Any bag that is over the weight limit will be charged extra. Also, no sharp objects are allowed in any carry-on bags. Please arrive at the airport three hours before the flight takes off.

Adam Where are you? We're going to be late for the flight! 14:39

14:40 I'm sorry! I got held up at work. I'm nearly home now. **Irene**

Adam Who cares about work at a time like this? Our flight leaves in three hours! 14:40

14:42 We've got lots of time. Even with traffic, we'll be at the airport by 15:40. **Irene**

Adam But I don't want to rush. 14:43

14:44 Don't worry. I think I'll still have lots of time to have my pre-flight drink and look around in the shops. ☺ **Irene**

1. Which of the following is NOT advised by Real Town Airport?

   A. Passengers should arrive at the airport early.

   B. Passengers should not carry dangerous items.

   C. Passengers should check how heavy their bags are.

   D. Passengers should leave their cars in the parking lot.

2. Why is Adam worried about getting to the airport on time?

   A. He doesn't want to have to hurry.

   B. He needs to do work at the airport.

   C. He hopes to go shopping at the airport.

   D. He wants to have a coffee at the airport.

3. Where are Adam and Irene flying to?

   A. Tokyo

   B. Manila

   C. Seoul

   D. Kuala Lumpur

CH
2

From: calendarplanet@calendarplanet.com

To: all.subscribers@calendarplanet.com

Subject: Special Deals

Hi!

Here at Calendar Planet, we know the joy that calendars bring. Even in today's world when we can easily check the date on our smartphones, there's nothing quite like turning over a new month on a real calendar. Today only, we're offering our members these special deals:

Buy a film star calendar and **SAVE $2** by entering "CP2"

Buy a music star calendar and **SAVE $4** by entering "CP4"

Buy a sports star calendar and **SAVE $6** by entering "CP6"

Buy a towns & villages calendar and **SAVE $8** by entering "CP8"

The Calendar Planet Team

---

https:// www.calendarplanet.com

Customer Reviews

I have bought calendars from your company for many years and they have always been good quality. Actually, the calendar I chose this year is even better than usual! The images of my favorite tennis player, Hsieh Shu-Wei, are excellent. I look forward to turning them over every month. Your prices are also very good, and it was a nice idea to offer your regular customers an extra saving. I certainly will buy calendars from you again!

Robert

1. Why does the email talk about smartphones?

   A. Many people use the calendar on their phones.

   B. Many people shop for calendars on their phones.

   C. The special deals are only available for phone orders.

   D. The most popular calendar includes pictures of phones.

2. What do we discover about Robert?

   A. He won't use Calendar Planet next year.

   B. He rarely buys goods from online stores.

   C. He plans to buy many different calendars.

   D. He has shopped at Calendar Planet before.

3. How much money did Robert save on his calendar?

   A. Two dollars

   B. Four dollars

   C. Six dollars

   D. Eight dollars

From: mail@mailmail.com

To: pmcnulty@mailmail.com

Subject: Welcome

Paul,

Sorry I can't be there for your first day on the job, for I'm taking some personal leave. However, I know the rest of the mailmen will look after you. If you have any questions, please ask them. Please see below for when and where you need to be. It is important to stick to these times.

Time	Street
7:00 a.m.	Lake Road
7:30 a.m.	Hill Road
8:00 a.m.	East Main Street
8:30 a.m.	West Main Street

See you later in the week.

Jimmy

Dear Rhonda,

Thank you very much for your letter. It came as a nice surprise when the mailman delivered it before I went out for my regular walk at seven fifteen this morning. I am glad you are having fun in Australia. It is a great idea to take a <u>break</u> between studying and starting work to see the world. Your grandmother would be so proud of the confident young woman you have become. Stay safe over there and keep in touch. I look forward to seeing your pictures when you come back.

Love, Grandpa

1. Who most likely is Jimmy?

   A. A worker in a paper factory

   B. The boss of a mail company

   C. An old university friend of Paul's

   D. One of Paul's regular customers

2. Why is Rhonda in Australia?

   A. She is starting a new job there.

   B. She is visiting her grandmother.

   C. She is studying for a degree there.

   D. She is visiting the country for fun.

3. Where does Rhonda's grandfather live?

   A. Lake Road

   B. Hill Road

   C. East Main Street

   D. West Main Street

常春藤全民英檢系列【G53-1】
GEPT 新制全民英檢初級　閱讀實戰力 Level Up!
（試題本）

總 編 審	賴世雄
終　　審	梁民康
執行編輯	許嘉華
編輯小組	施盈如・區光銳・Nick Roden・Brian Foden
設計組長	王玥琦
封面設計	胡毓芸
排版設計	林桂旭・王穎緁
法律顧問	北辰著作權事務所蕭雄淋律師
出 版 者	常春藤有聲出版股份有限公司
地　　址	臺北市忠孝西路一段 33 號 5 樓
電　　話	(02) 2331-7600
傳　　真	(02) 2381-0918
網　　址	www.ivy.com.tw
電子信箱	service@ivy.com.tw
郵政劃撥	19714777
戶　　名	常春藤有聲出版股份有限公司
定　　價	420 元（2 書）

100009 臺北市忠孝西路一段 33 號 5 樓

常春藤有聲出版股份有限公司　行政組　啟

讀者問卷【G53】

GEPT 新制全民英檢初級　閱讀實戰力 Level Up!
（試題本 + 詳解本）

感謝您購買本書！為使我們對讀者的服務能夠更加完善，請您詳細填寫本問卷各欄後，寄回本公司或傳真至（02）2381-0918，**或掃描 QR Code 填寫線上問卷**，我們將於收到後七個工作天內贈送「常春藤網路書城熊贈點 50 點（一點 = 一元，使用期限 90 天）」給您（每書每人限贈一次），也懇請您繼續支持。若有任何疑問，請儘速與客服人員聯絡，客服電話：（02）2331-7600 分機 11～13，謝謝您！

線上填寫
免郵寄最環保

姓　　名：＿＿＿＿＿＿＿　性別：＿＿＿＿　生日：＿＿＿年＿＿月＿＿日

聯絡電話：＿＿＿＿＿＿＿　**E-mail**：＿＿＿＿＿＿＿＿＿＿＿＿＿＿

聯絡地址：□□□□□□＿＿＿＿＿＿＿＿＿＿＿＿＿＿＿＿＿＿＿＿

＿＿＿＿＿＿＿＿＿＿＿＿＿＿＿＿＿＿＿＿＿＿＿＿＿＿

教育程度：□國小　□國中　□高中　□大專 / 大學　□研究所含以上

職　　業：1 □學生

　　　　　2 □社會人士：□工　□商　□服務業　□軍警公職　□教職　□其他＿＿＿＿

1 您從何處得知本書：□書店　□常春藤網路書城　□FB / IG / Line@ 社群平臺推薦　□學校購買　□親友推薦　□常春藤雜誌　□其他＿＿＿＿＿＿＿＿

2 您購得本書的管道：□書店　□常春藤網路書城　□博客來　□其他＿＿＿＿＿＿

3 最滿意本書的特點依序是（限定三項）：□試題演練　□字詞解析　□內容　□編排方式　□印刷　□封面　□售價　□信任品牌　□其他＿＿＿＿＿＿＿＿＿

4 您對本書建議改進的三點依序是：□無（都很滿意）□試題演練　□字詞解析　□內容　□編排方式　□印刷　□封面　□售價　□其他＿＿＿＿＿＿＿＿＿

　原因：＿＿＿＿＿＿＿＿＿＿＿＿＿＿＿＿＿＿＿＿＿＿＿＿＿＿＿＿＿＿＿

　對本書的其他建議：＿＿＿＿＿＿＿＿＿＿＿＿＿＿＿＿＿＿＿＿＿＿＿＿

5 希望我們出版哪些主題的書籍：＿＿＿＿＿＿＿＿＿＿＿＿＿＿＿＿＿＿＿

6 若您發現本書誤植的部分，請告知在：書籍第＿＿＿＿＿頁，第＿＿＿＿＿行

　有錯誤的部分是：＿＿＿＿＿＿＿＿＿＿＿＿＿＿＿＿＿＿＿＿＿＿＿＿＿

7 對我們的其他建議：＿＿＿＿＿＿＿＿＿＿＿＿＿＿＿＿＿＿＿＿＿＿＿